leapfrog

Mr Spotty's
Potty

First published in 2000
Franklin Watts
96 Leonard Street
London
EC2A 4XD

Franklin Watts Australia
45-51 Huntley Street
Alexandria
NSW 2015

A CIP catalogue record for this book is available
from the British Library.

ISBN 0 7496 3711 0 (hbk)
ISBN 0 7496 3831 1 (pbk)

Series Editor: Louise John
Series Advisor: Dr Barrie Wade
Series Designer: Jason Anscomb

Printed in China

For Agnes, who heard it first – H.R

For Janet, Graeme and Victoria – P.U

Mr Spotty's Potty

by Hilary Robinson

Illustrated by Peter Utton

FRANKLIN WATTS
LONDON•SYDNEY

Mr Spotty's potty
sits by his front door.

He puts lots of seeds
in it ...

... and waits for rain
to pour.

Dot, his dog, just nods
at people who go by.

They stop and look
at all the flowers ...

... that grow up to the sky.

One day, Dot got fed up
just sitting by the door.

She got up and went inside ...

... and sat upon the floor.

That day, when
big drops of rain
fell down ...

... the flowers, they did
not grow.

"Why?" said Mr Spotty.

"I really do not know!"

He took the potty
in the house and
put it down by Dot.

"They will not grow in here," he said.

"The room is much too hot!"

But grow they did,
up and up ...

... and then they did
not stop.

They grew up two floors
of the house ...

... and up and out the top.

Then Mr Spotty knew,
as it was plain to see ...

That Dot would use
the potty ...

... to do a little wee!

Leapfrog has been specially designed to fit the requirements of the National Literacy Strategy. It offers real books for beginning readers by top authors and illustrators.

There are 31 Leapfrog stories to choose from: